GRANDPA & ME
we learn about death

MARLEE & BEN ALEX

Photos by Ben Alex and Otto Wikkelsoe

BETHANY HOUSE PUBLISHERS
MINNEAPOLIS, MINNESOTA 55438
A Division of Bethany Fellowship, Inc.

Co-published by Forlaget Scandinavia, Copenhagen, Denmark, and by
Bethany House Publishers, Minneapolis, Minnesota, for the U.S.A. and Canada.

Text copyright © 1982, Bethany House Publishers
Photos copyright © 1981, Forlaget Scandinavia, Copenhagen

ISBN 0-87123-257-x

An Angus Hudson co-production   Printed in England

GRANDPA & ME is a book for children on the subject of death. We hope this book will help to integrate this serious but important topic into family life and conversation in a natural way. The book is written from a Christian viewpoint, and the story presents hope and eternal truth for families and, particularly, for children.

Our special thanks to Henny and Viggo Walsoe (Grandma and Grandpa), and to Maria who was inexhaustible in our attempts to capture the right pictures. Thanks also to Jorgen Vium Olesen, who along the way has given us much counsel on this project.

Marlee and Ben

"Hi, Maria!" Grandpa was standing by the roadside chuckling as Maria jumped off the bus.

Grandma tried to catch her breath. "Welcome to the country!" she said. "My, how big you've grown!"

Oh, how happy Maria felt inside when she saw Grandpa and Grandma! She gave each of them a big hug.

Grandpa and Grandma were her very best friends. Grandpa could do just about anything. And Grandma made the world's best pancakes. Maria had come to visit them during her Easter vacation. She was going to be there for a week.

Inside Maria was bubbling with excitement.

Maria couldn't wait to try the swing Grandpa had made last year. Before she went into their house, she ran over and jumped on it. She was swinging higher and higher until the trees and house seemed to swim around her.

"Watch me, Grandma!" shouted Maria.

Maria changed into play clothes and joined Grandpa and Grandma in the kitchen. "Do you like fried chicken and mashed potatoes?" asked Grandma. Maria loved fried chicken and mashed potatoes—especially with a pool of butter right in the middle of the potatoes.

Grandpa lifted Maria up on his lap. "You mean to tell me that we will have this little mischief-maker here for a *whole week*?" he teased. This was his way of showing how happy he was to have her here on the farm. He tickled her, and Maria wiggled and squealed until she nearly fell on the floor. Grandma smiled at them. "You two be careful, now, or I'll have to send both of you out-of-doors!" Grandma could tease, too.

Grandma decided that Maria should sleep in the bedroom right next to theirs. The blankets on the big bed were soft and fluffy. Maria could easily hide down underneath them where Grandpa couldn't find her. Maria's teddy bear liked the soft blankets, too.

Grandma sang a good-night song with Maria. Afterward she said the Lord's Prayer. She always did that.

As Maria snuggled down under the covers, she couldn't help thinking about everything she and Grandpa were going to do tomorrow on the farm.

The sun was shining brightly the next morning. Maria jumped out of bed and ran to find Grandpa. Out in the sheepfold the sheep were more afraid of Maria than she was of them, and they ran away from her. She watched as some of the little lambs drank milk from their mother. Suddenly Maria heard someone behind her.

"So! There you are, you little sleepyhead! Turn around and let me see you. Have you washed your face yet this morning?" Grandpa gave Maria a hug. "Come on. You'll have to help me give all the animals breakfast."

"Why are the sheep so fat? Have they been eating too much?" Maria asked.

"Oh, no! They don't eat too much! All they need is a little grass and some pellets once in a while. Hey, look here! Here's a special sheep with horns. It's called a ram. He's extra big, but he gives lots of wool." Maria stretched her hand carefully to pet the ram. Oh, how dirty and greasy he was!

"In a week or so we'll clip the wool from all the sheep," said Grandpa as they walked on. "Then it will be sent to a factory where they'll make yarn out of it."

"The sheep should at least have a bath before they are clipped," said Maria, wrinkling up her nose.

The cows were so busy eating that they didn't even notice Maria and Grandpa. "Tonight you can help me milk the cows," Grandpa promised. Maria thought it was strange that brown cows who ate green grass could give white milk.

"Cows chew the grass two times," continued Grandpa. "The first time, they swallow the grass. Then it comes up again and they chew it a second time. That's why cows look so lazy. They're usually lying around and chomping."

The chicken coop was full of activity. Maria came with grain and all the chickens came running. Grandpa went after the big watering can and poured out fresh water in their pan. While the chickens were busy hunting and pecking, Maria and Grandpa crept quietly into the hen house. And, sure enough! There lay two eggs in one nest and one egg in another. One of the eggs was still warm. Grandpa laid them carefully in his hat.

"How do all those big eggs come out of the little chicken?" asked Maria.

"I'll admit, it's hard to understand," said Grandpa. "But it just so happens that while the egg is still in the chicken, it's soft, without a shell on it. The shell is formed at the moment it's ready to come out. There's an opening at the back of the chicken where the egg is pushed out when it's ready."

"Honk! Honk!"

The geese waddled around each other when Grandpa and Maria came close to them with the bucket of feed.

"They aren't very old. But by Christmas they'll be big and fat!" said Grandpa.

Maria felt sorry for the geese, to think they would be someone's Christmas dinner one day.

"Yes-sir-eee!" added Grandpa. "They also give us down and feathers for our pillows."

"Honk! Honk!" answered the geese as they hopped out into the pond.

13

"Now let's see if we can find Mother Cat!" suggested Grandpa. "She has three new kittens. I think they're hiding up in the hay." Grandpa and Maria crawled up in the hayloft, but they did not find the kittens. "Oh, well, we'll have to wait till they come out by themselves," said Grandpa. So they crawled back down into the barn.

They started to clean out the pigpens and put in some new hay. They also had to bring in one of the sheep. It was sick and would have to stay inside today.

"It probably just has a cold," said Maria.

There were so many things to see and do on the farm. The hours flew by. Before Maria knew it, the day was almost over.

It had been a big day. Maria had seen so many new things. Before suppertime, Grandpa suggested they go for a walk in the sheepfold and see how the fence was holding up. Grandpa's hand felt big and strong. Maria wasn't afraid of the sheep anymore. "It's been a fun day, Grandpa!"

Grandpa nodded. They had become good buddies. He squeezed her hand while they walked over the hill. Then he stopped and blew his nose. "Are you crying, Grandpa?" "Sometimes I cry, Maria, when I'm real happy."

"I'm happy, too, Grandpa," Maria said as he took her hand and walked on.

Before they went to bed, all three sat at the dining room table. Grandpa took a very big book down from a shelf. He read to them about Jesus and His resurrection. Grandpa explained that this meant Jesus rose from the grave. Grandpa closed the book and bowed his head. Maria and Grandma bowed their heads, too.

"Tick, tock!" Maria's eyes were heavy.

The old grandfather's clock was the only thing she could hear. All the animals had gone to bed. Then Grandpa carried Maria up to bed. Her warm bed felt so good!

17

Next morning when Maria woke up, the flowers in the field outside her bedroom window looked like sunshine sprinkled across the grass. Maria hurried out to find Grandpa.

She saw him coming out of the barn.

"There you are, Sleepyhead!" he said.

Grandpa carried something in his big hand. Maria saw that it was a furry, gray kitten. "Look, Grandpa! It's sleeping! It's soooo soft!"

"It's not sleeping, Maria. It's dead. I found it alone up in the hay."

"Dead?" asked Maria. "Isn't it sleeping?"

"No, it's not alive anymore."

"Well, I think it's just sleeping," Maria said. "If we lay it here in the sun and get it some milk, it'll probably wake up again."

"No, Maria, I'm afraid it won't wake up again. Let's bury it out in the garden."

In the workshop Grandpa made a tiny box for the kitten. Then he went outside to look for a place to bury it.

"Here's a good place," said Grandpa.

"Be careful! Don't put anything over his eyes, or else the kitty can't see," said Maria.

Grandpa laid the kitten down in the box together with some wildflowers. Then he dug a hole, laid the box down in it and covered the whole thing up with dirt. Maria put more flowers on the grave. All around the grave she made a rim of small rocks.

"You see, Maria, when something dies, it never comes back again."

Maria sat very still and looked down at the small grave. She felt sad that the kitty would never come back again.

As they were finishing, the mother cat ran up and sniffed curiously at the grave. She sniffed at the flowers as if she wanted to be sure that her little kitten had been buried properly.

"Meoooow!" Mother Cat said good-bye to her kitten.

21

Maria had a lot to think about.

"Do you *like* to die, Grandpa?"

"Well, now, I don't know," laughed Grandpa. "I've never tried it. I don't think anyone *likes* to die. But you know, God has a special plan for His children. And He gave us the seasons to show that death is not the end for us. Think about the trees. In the winter, new buds are made where the old leaves have fallen off. In spring, the buds open out. That's the way it will be someday when I die. I'll start a new kind of life with God."

"When can we dig the kitten up again?" asked Maria.

"We can't do that. The kitten slowly will be changed into earth, just like the leaves that fall in the forest. They wither away and lie on the ground. Eventually they become like dirt. So will the kitten."

"I don't want to die!" said Maria, and she shuddered as she thought of the dark earth where they had put the kitten.

"See," said Grandpa, "let's plant these flower seeds on the kitten's grave."

23

The days passed quickly. Maria learned many more new things. Grandma taught her to bake bread. Grandpa taught her to make a flute of bamboo, and to walk on stilts.

Maria's visit was over. Grandpa and Maria walked through the garden on the way to the bus.

"Look," he said, "the seeds we planted on the kitten's grave are starting to sprout and come up out of the earth. It won't be long before they are really big. Next time you come, there'll be flowers on them."

"Come, Maria!" called Grandma. "The bus is coming!"

Maria ran up to the house and to Grandma with the flowers she had picked.

"Good-bye, Grandma!" she said and gave her the flowers.

Grandpa took her to the door of the bus.

Back home again, Maria told her family all about the things she had learned.

One day when she came home from school, Mommy said to her. "Grandpa has become sick. He is in the hospital here in town. We're going to visit him this afternoon."

Maria looked forward to seeing Grandpa again.

"What's it like at the hospital, Mommy?"

"There are nurses and doctors to take care of Grandpa. He needs someone to watch over him carefully now."

"Why is Grandpa sick?"

"Grandpa is getting old now, Maria. When you're old, you get sick easier.

Maria thought about all the animals and about Grandpa and Grandma.

"Come on now, Maria, eat!" said Mommy. "You're sitting dreaming!"

Maria thought about the kitten and wondered if it was still dead. It probably was. Grandpa had said that it would lie in the grave and be changed to earth. She wondered how the other kittens looked now. They had probably gotten so big that they went alone out to the barn and the sheepfold.

"Eat, Maria!" said Mommy.

At the hospital everything was white. Grandpa lay completely still in his bed. He could turn his head a little and smile at Maria.

"Hello, Maria!" he said quietly.

Grandpa's hand came out from under the blankets and reached for Maria's hand.

Maria looked at Grandpa for a long time.

"Are you going to die, Grandpa?"

"I'm not afraid of death, Maria."

"I don't want you to die."

"But we believe in the resurrection," whispered Grandpa.

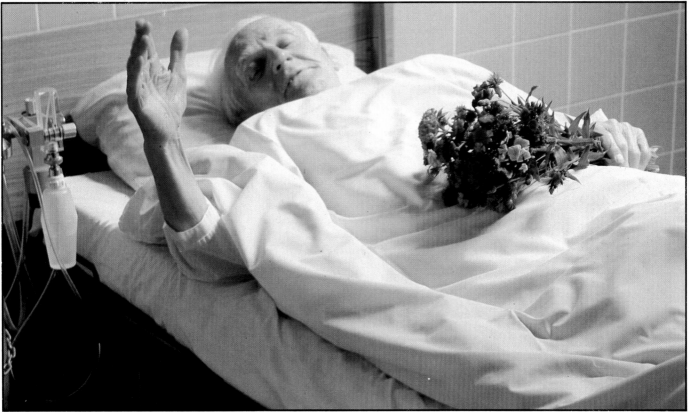

When Grandpa said that long word, *resurrection,* Maria remembered what Grandpa had read from that big Book. She remembered about how Jesus rose from the dead so that we could have eternal life.

Grandpa looked very tired. He closed his eyes for a moment. Then he opened them again and looked at Maria. She squeezed Grandpa's hand, then drew it back and smoothed the blanket out.

"Bye, Grandpa," said Maria.

A few days later, a message came from the hospital that Grandpa had died. That evening at bedtime, Maria got out her toy farm. She moved the animals around. But nothing seemed to fit. Mommy came to tuck her in.

"Do you think that Grandpa and the kitten can see me now?" she asked.

"I don't know," said Mommy. "Maybe Grandpa can, but I don't think the kitten can."

Maria felt sad when she laid her head on the pillow. She held her teddy bear close. Neither Mommy nor Maria felt like reading or singing together, but they decided that Grandpa would want them to do it anyway. Mommy prayed longer than usual.

That night Maria dreamed about Grandpa.

A month later Maria's school closed for the summer. She was going to spend some time on the farm with Grandma.

It was good to see Grandma again. But when she saw Grandpa's big chair over in the corner as it always had been, a sad feeling grew inside her. It was so empty without him.

"Mommy says that Grandpa is not coming back anymore," said Maria.

"No," said Grandma as she looked around.

"It's awfully quiet around here now without him." Maria went out to the animals. She had looked forward to seeing them all again.

But seeing them made Maria feel even sadder inside.

"It's okay to cry, Maria!" Grandma said. "I've cried from missing Grandpa. It helps."

Maria held the mother cat for a long time. She remembered back to the time when it had lost its little kitten. She and Grandpa had buried the kitten in the garden. Grandma sat down beside Maria and began to tell her about Grandpa's funeral and how he was buried in the cemetery.

"Won't we see Grandpa anymore?" asked Maria.

"No, we won't see Grandpa anymore on this earth. His old body was buried in the cemetery. But the part of Grandpa we loved the most, his spirit, is living with God."

"Does it hurt to die, Grandma?"

"Well, maybe sometimes. But it didn't hurt Grandpa. And if it did, he doesn't remember it now because everything is so beautiful in heaven. And someday God will give him a brand-new body that will never get old or sick again."

"Why does God let people die?" asked Maria.

"Well, it wasn't part of God's plan when He created us. Sin is the cause of death. Death reminds us how much we need God. And God showed us how much He loved us by sending Jesus. If we believe in Him, our spirit will go on living after our bodies have died."

"Is Grandpa an angel, then?"

"No, he's not an angel, Maria. But he's living with the angels and all those who also believed in God while they lived on this earth."

"How did Grandpa get up to heaven?"

"It's just like if you lived in an old house that was ready to crumble away and fall into pieces. And then your big strong Daddy came and picked you up and carried you out of that house to a wonderful new house. That's what our heavenly Father did for Grandpa."

"What is heaven like, Grandma?"

"It's light and bright and full of love. In heaven we will always be together with Jesus and God. And, you know what? There won't be any sadness or death anymore."

"Can I also go to heaven?" Maria asked.

"Yes, God has prepared a place for you and me, too. And Grandpa will be there waiting for us!"

Maria had a lot to think about. In the little meadow where she and Grandpa had often walked together, she sat and wondered about all that Grandma had told her. She also remembered Grandpa's last words in the hospital: "But we believe in the resurrection!"

That afternoon, as the sun went down on the other side of the meadow, Maria said a prayer:

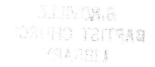

40

DEAR GOD!
GRANDMA SAYS
YOU HAVE GRAND-
PA WITH YOU. I
HOPE YOU TAKE
GOOD CARE OF
HIM.
I'M GLAD YOU MADE
HEAVEN SO THAT
WE DO NOT HAVE TO
FEEL SO SAD.
GRANDMA SAYS YOU
WROTE IN THE BIBLE
THAT YOU ARE
BUILDING A HOUSE FOR
EVERYBODY WHO
BELIEVES IN YOU.
GOD, I BELIEVE IN
YOU!

42

"I am the resurrection, and he that believes in me, though he were dead, yet shall he live!"

John 11:25

Date Due

8-25